Silly Milly
and the
Mysterious Suitcase

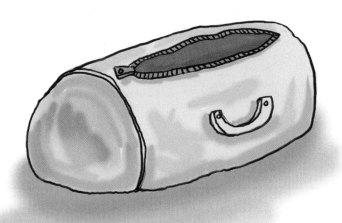

For my amazing grandchildren, Josh and Leah,
who love mysterious things.
—W. C. L.

For Seamus.
—N. B. W.

Text copyright © 2011 by Wendy Lewison
Illustrations copyright © 2011 by Nadine Bernard Westcott, Inc.

All rights reserved. Published by Scholastic Inc.
SCHOLASTIC, CARTWHEEL BOOKS, and associated logos
are trademarks and/or registered trademarks of Scholastic Inc.
Lexile is a registered trademark of MetaMetrics, Inc.

ISBN 978-0-545-34969-7

10 9 8 7 6 5 4 3 2 1   11 12 13 14 15/0

Printed in the U.S.A. 40 • First printing, September 2011

Silly Milly
and the
Mysterious Suitcase

SCHOLASTIC READER
LEVEL 1
50-250 WORDS

By Wendy Cheyette Lewison
Illustrated by Nadine Bernard Westcott

Cartwheel
·B·O·O·K·S·®

SCHOLASTIC INC.
New York Toronto London Auckland
Sydney Mexico City New Delhi Hong Kong

Miss Milly is taking a trip.
Oh my!
She packs silly things.
Can you guess why?

She packs a snowman,
round and fat.

She packs a baseball,
but not a bat.

She packs a rowboat,
but not a canoe.
And then she packs
a sailboat, too.

She packs some goldfish—
eight, nine, ten.
When they jump out . . .

. . . she packs them again.

She packs a hotdog,
but not the bun.

She packs two cupcakes
and then eats one.

She packs shoelaces,
but not her shoes.

She packs a newspaper.
It has no news.

She packs the doormat
from the floor.

She packs the doorknob,
but not the door.

She packs a notebook,
but not a pen.

And do you know
what she does then?

She finds a beehive in a tree
and packs that, too.
Oh my! Oh me!

She packs some popcorn
from the shelf.

And when she is done,
she packs herself!

Silly Miss Milly
in her frilly hat!
**Can you tell why
she packs like that?**